George's Onion Bog

The Lake

Deep Forest

The Big Oak

Sheep

Grazing Land

Wild Peppers

The Well

The Village

Farm Country

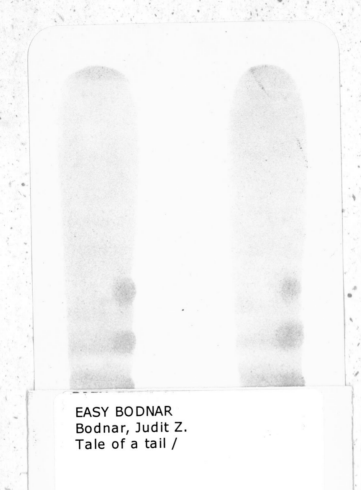

W 10/00   W 8/07   W 7/10

TALE OF A TAIL

JUDIT Z. BODNÁR

ILLUSTRATED BY

JOHN SANDFORD

LOTHROP, LEE & SHEPARD BOOKS ❧ MORROW
New York

To Chalcedony,
the true belletrist
—J. Z. B.

For brother George
—J. S.

Once there was...

...or once there wasn't...

There was once a fox. Like all foxes, he was very greedy and thought himself a very clever creature.

More than anything else in the world—more than tender spring biddies from the henhouse, more than juicy red raspberries in summertime— that fox loved to eat fish.

Late one winter afternoon, he caught a whole basketful of trout. His nose twitched and his mouth watered as he tied the basket to his back and trotted home.

The moment he set the basket on the table, he reached in and—*hom-hom*—gobbled down a few luscious fish. Then he built himself a fire and set out his plate and fork, just the way his old mother had taught him.

He had just sat down to enjoy his feast when—*kop-kop-kop*—there came a knock at the door. "Oh, blast," muttered the fox.

"Go away, I'm busy," he called.

"What an enticing odor, my friend," said a too-familiar voice. A bear poked the tip of his big black nose in the door and sniffed. "*Tyuhh!* Now, these are what I call *fish*! Give me some, won't you? I have an awwfulll longing for fisssh."

"Go away, I'm sleeping," said the fox.

"What sort of welcome is that for your best friend?" wheedled the bear.

"You are welcome to hang your hunger on a hat rack, 'friend.' It took me hours to catch these fish! I didn't do all that work to fill *your* belly!"

But the bear hadn't seen even a fingerling since summer, and the fox's den smelled as though it was piled to the rafters with fish.

He knocked again. *Kop-kop-kop.*

"I beg you, friend, show me how you caught them," he pleaded. Then, thinking he was as clever as any fox, he added, "I have no idea how to catch fish."

"Imagine a bear who can't even catch fish!" grumbled the fox. He added a log to the fire, then grinned.

"My *very* best friend, Sir Bear," he called. "You want to eat fish, do you? Then go directly to the lake. Go this very evening, when dusk has fallen and the fish won't recognize you." The fox chuckled softly. "Hang your tail in the water and don't twitch a muscle. When the sun smiles above the treetops, give your tail a good strong yank."

The bear scratched his ear. "Why?" he asked.

"*Why?* There never was anything better for a fishing pole than a bear's tail. You'll pull a whole barrelful of fish out of the lake—and without even getting your toes wet!"

And the fox banked the fire even higher and sat down to enjoy his supper alone.

The bear didn't want to leave all those aromatic
fish behind. Still, he thanked the fox politely and
trotted away toward the woods. He soon stood
beside the lake, licking his lips and humming a
fishing tune.

"Perfect!" he thought. "I'm just in time. The sun
has fallen asleep and the moon is only a nail paring.
The fish will never even know I'm here."

He lumbered to the edge of the water and stuck
his tail in as deep as it would go. Then he waited.

That night, such a chill wind blew over the plain that the bear's tongue nearly froze to the roof of his mouth. His thick brown coat turned white with frost as he sat beside the lapping water.

He waited. He shivered. The wind moaned, and the night dragged on. The lake became a frothy sheet of solid ice. The bear slapped his thighs and blew on his paws and waited for the fish to bite.

At dawn, he could bear the aching cold no longer.
"Friend Fox is very kind to teach me a new way
to fish," he thought. "But I want to go home now."

When the bear tried to step away from the lake,
he howled in pain. His tail was trapped in the ice!
He tugged and tugged, but it was stuck fast.
Higher and higher rose the sun. Harder and harder
tugged the bear.

"All right, fish," he cried at last. "You and I are
leaving...now!" He gathered all his strength and
gave a mighty heave.

Ai-yai-yai! That poor bear! He tore the lake right out of its bed—but he saw not a single fish on his tail. All he saw was ice.

That lake was heavier than ten blacksmiths' anvils! The bear's back felt as if it were broken, his tail as though it had been torn right off. He hopped on his left foot, then his right, and he roared.

When he thought of the fox, surrounded by heaps of tasty fish shining in the firelight, he roared even louder. He had a thing or two to say to that friend of his!

The bear stomped away, with the frozen lake in tow.

The sun rose higher still, and the bear's icy fur began to thaw. The lake gleamed, shivering the light, and soon began to drip. With every step, the bear heard *drip-drip-plop*. But he did not look back. He just kept on, hobbling toward that wicked fox's den.

At last he reached the woods. *Drip-drip-plop.* The bear took three strides into the trees and felt an *awful* yank on his poor, sore tail.

"*Ai-yai-yaieee!*" he cried.

That lake of ice would not fit between the trees. He tugged and pulled and struggled.

Drip-drip-plop. Tug. "*AI-YAI-YAIEEE!*"

"Just you wait, Fox," roared the bear. "My very best friend, indeed!" He sat down in a puddle and thought dark thoughts. *Drip-drip-plop. Drip-drip-PLOP!* At last he turned his head.

There behind him, on the very path he had followed, was a little stream. And gleaming and wriggling in the shallow water, the bear saw *fish*! Dozens of lovely shimmering fish. Hundreds of smelly, fresh, delicious fish. More fish than he could count.

"Oh, Fox, my very best friend INDEED!" he shouted.

The bear leaped and spun. He slapped his tail against the trees, and the ice shattered into a million sparkling slivers. The bear's paw flashed out. Three frozen mackerel were caught on his long, curved claws. He popped them into his mouth—*hop-la*—and swallowed them in a single gulp—*hom-hom*.

It took the bear three days to eat all those fish.
When he had finished, he was so full and sleepy that
he could barely walk. His belly dragged the ground as he
waddled home, and his tail barely pained him at all.

The bear was much too tired to stop anywhere along the way. But, polite as ever, he dropped a note in the mail before he fell into bed.

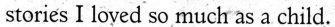

A Note from the Author

When my family moved to the United States and I started school,
my mother and I knew no English. So the stories my parents told me in my
native language gave me special comfort in a new, strange world. *Tale of a Tail*
is inspired by one of those tellings. Although I have told it in English,
of course, I've tried to keep the rhythm and flavor of the Hungarian
stories I loved so much as a child.

The artist thanks Pannonia Books, Toronto, Canada, for their kind help.

Oil paints were used for the full-color illustrations.
The text type is 18-point Italian Old Style.

Published by Lothrop, Lee & Shepard Books
an imprint of Morrow Junior Books
a division of William Morrow and Company, Inc.
1350 Avenue of the Americas, New York, NY 10019
www.williammorrow.com

Printed in Hong Kong by South China Printing Company (1988) Ltd.

10 9 8 7 6 5 4 3 2 1

Library of Congress Cataloging-in-Publication Data
Bodnár, Judit Z.
Tale of a tail / Judit Bodnár; illustrated by John Sandford.
p. cm.
Summary: Not wishing to share his fish with Bear, Fox slyly directs him
how to catch his own, not realizing the extraordinary event that would result.
ISBN 0-688-12174-8 (trade)—ISBN 0-688-12175-6 (library)
[1. Bears—Fiction. 2. Foxes—Fiction. 3. Fishing—Fiction.]
I. Sandford, John, ill. II. Title. PZ7.B635712Fo 1998
[E]—DC20 93-19046 CIP AC

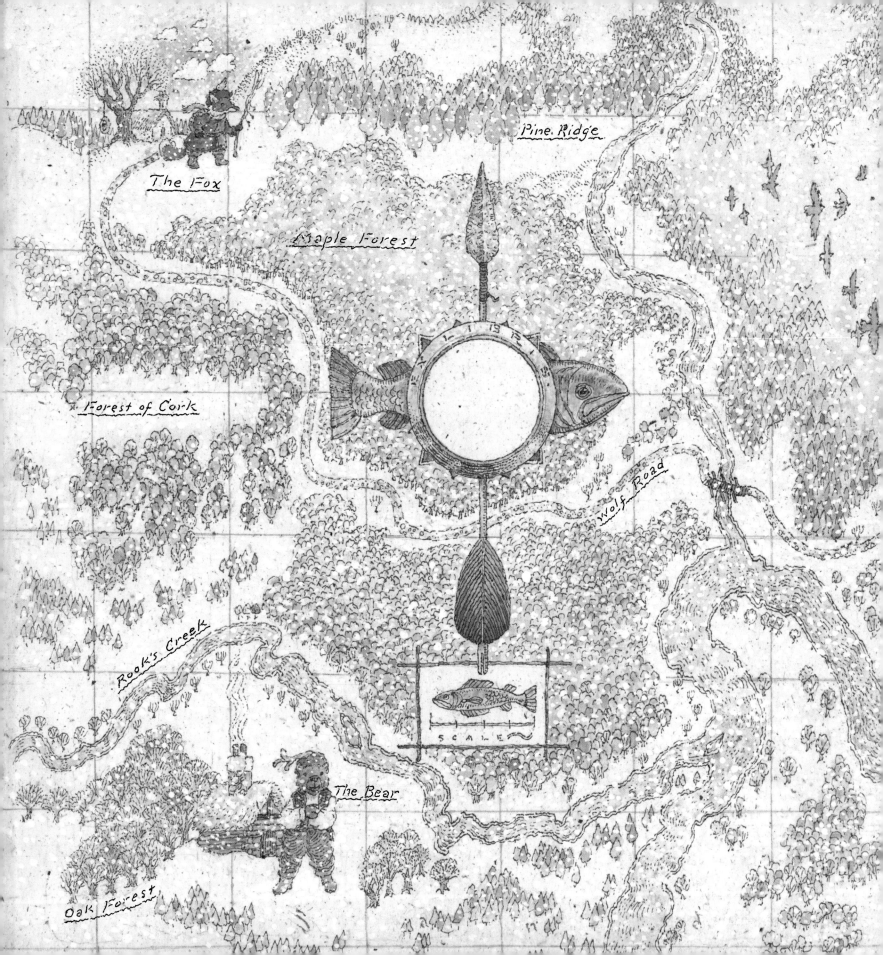